KILL BOX CHECKMATE

FROM THE WORLD OF LIZZY BALLARD

A LOUISE MORTENSEN THRILLER NOVELLA

MATTY DALRYMPLE

WILLIAM KINGSFIELD PUBLISHERS

Dedicated to all the Friends of Lizzy Ballard ... especially those who sometimes find themselves rooting for Louise Mortensen.

Kill box checkmate: The queen and a rook work together to checkmate the enemy king. The king has no escape due to being on the edge of the board or to being blocked by friendly or enemy pieces.

Endgame Essentials: Navigating to Checkmate by Will Fielding

QUEEN AND ROOK BATTERY

In queen and rook battery, the queen and rook coordinate to threaten and attack the opponent's pieces. The combination of the queen's power and the rook's ability to control the movement of opposing pieces creates tactical opportunities.

Endgame Essentials: Navigating to Checkmate by Will Fielding

1

———

Louise Mortensen stood at the door of the lab, watching Lucas and Maja hurry toward her up the path from the main house, their figures moving in and out of the shadows cast by the tree branches waving in the light spring breeze. Behind Louise stood Edmund Rinnert, almost manic with nerves. On the floor lay Theo Viklund, dead.

"They're going to kill us," moaned Edmund.

"Not if we don't give them a reason to," said Louise, trying to keep her voice steady. *Not yet, in any case.*

She had promised Edmund, her lab assistant, that if her plan to free the two of them from their now-dead jailor backfired, she would do her best to protect him. Would his lack of nerves be what scuttled her plan?

She stepped aside as Maja and Lucas reached the door.

"What is it, Doctor Mortensen?" Theo's housekeeper asked, her words heavy with the Swedish accent common to all the members of Viklund's staff.

Louise gestured to the body. "Theo collapsed."

Lucas, Theo's head of security, pushed past Maja and

Louise. He knelt next to the body and pressed his fingers to the side of Theo's neck. After a few moments, he said in the same accent as Maja's, "No pulse."

"No," agreed Louise.

"Did you try CPR?" he asked.

"No."

Lucas glanced at Edmund.

"I didn't," said Edmund, his voice as strained as an over-tightened guitar string.

Louise wondered if Lucas would administer CPR himself. She was relieved when he got to his feet without bothering.

"What happened?" he asked, resettling his sport coat on his broad shoulders.

"I have no idea."

"You're a doctor."

"I'm not *his* doctor."

"Ironic that you and Rinnert were here when it happened."

"Ironic? I don't think so. Coincidental? Perhaps."

Lucas's eyes scanned the room and landed on the teapot and two cups on the lab table. "You were drinking tea?"

"Yes."

"If I sent Herr Viklund's cup out to have the contents tested, would there be anything unusual in the results?"

Louise waved toward the shards of china lying on the floor. "First, you'd have to gather up the pieces." She crossed her arms. "Then you'd have to find somewhere to send it. Not likely to call in the police, I imagine."

Lucas scowled. "Not the police, perhaps. But there are other resources—"

"I'm sure there are, but what would you do—lock me and Edmund here in the lab until you get the results back in, what, days? Weeks?"

"I'll do what I need to do to find out what happened to Herr Viklund."

Edmund's voice was almost a squawk. "But—"

Not taking her eyes off Lucas, Louise silenced Edmund with a slash of her hand. "Let's not be hasty, Lucas. In fact, let's play out this scenario. I can't blame you for wondering if foul play was involved in Theo's death—" Louise wished Edmund would stop distracting her with his fidgeting. "—but consider your options carefully. You could punish me, but to what end? To avenge your employer's death? And after all, Theo thought me valuable enough to go to considerable trouble to ensure I stayed at the compound," she raised an eyebrow, "as you well know."

"Herr Viklund might have considered you valuable," replied Lucas, "but I don't see how that should influence my course of action now that he's dead."

Louise tucked a strand of auburn hair, threaded with silver, behind her ear. "Theo's death doesn't diminish my value. It just means that different people might now benefit from that value. I feel confident that you and I ..." She shifted her gaze to include Maja. "... in fact, that *all* of us could benefit from the value I bring." She gestured toward Edmund. "And that Doctor Rinnert brings, of course."

"And how do you propose that we do that?" asked Lucas, in a monotone that didn't indicate whether he was interested in what she was saying or feeding her enough rope to hang herself.

"To begin with, whatever incentive Theo offered to keep you in his employ can continue—even increase." She looked toward Maja, whose fingers were twisted in front of her. "For both of you." Louise redirected her attention back to Lucas. "If you decide to punish me for what happened to Theo, and if the punishment is death, that choice is irreversible." She forced herself to pause. In her peripheral vision, she could see Maja pulling her shapeless cardigan more closely around her stout body, her gaze shifting between Louise and Lucas. "On the other hand, if you decide to postpone any action and see how events develop, you leave your options open ... and can take whatever steps you deem necessary if the developments aren't to your satisfaction."

Lucas's expression continued to be unreadable.

Louise obviously wasn't going to get any indicators of whether her argument was having its desired effect. She needed to bring the conversation to a head. "You could kill me based on your suspicions about Theo's death, or ..." She drew the word out speculatively. "... you could accept that Theo's death is exactly what it looks like: the tragic result of some undiagnosed medical condition."

Lucas looked from Louise to Edmund and back.

Louise's eyes didn't leave Lucas's face.

She was betting that Theo Viklund was not a man who had engendered anything more than enforced loyalty among his staff. She was confident she could win Maja to her side. Louise remembered with gratitude Maja draping her cardigan over Louise's shivering shoulders in Viklund's well-equipped medical dispensary as Louise awaited her punishment for trying to escape the compound. With Maja as an ally, the household staff would fall in line.

The wildcard was Lucas. Louise didn't need him to believe that Theo had died of natural causes. She just needed him to acknowledge that there was no benefit to hasty action. She was confident—fairly confident—that if she could survive the next few minutes, she could discover the price for Lucas's loyalty, then pay him double.

But Lucas was one of the two men who had recaptured Louise when she tried to escape. He had escorted her to the dispensary, where Theo had shown her the scalpel he had used to amputate Edmund's thumb when Edmund made his own escape attempt, long before Louise's arrival at the compound. The room where Theo promised Louise he wouldn't hesitate to use the scalpel on her should she make another attempt.

Louise had never been as terrified as she had been in that bland, sterile room. Not until now.

The difference was that now she was quite sure nothing in her demeanor gave away her terror: not a twitch of her fingers or a tremble in her voice.

An eternity seemed to pass, then Lucas shifted his gaze to Theo's body. "I recall him mentioning he had heart trouble."

Slowly, and she hoped inaudibly, she let out the breath she had been holding. She glanced toward Maja, who gave her a barely perceptible nod.

Louise spared a glance at Edmund. He was supporting himself on the back of one of the lab chairs, his expression slack with relief.

She returned her attention to Lucas. "I see no reason to inform the staff of the situation immediately. Do you?"

He rubbed his neck. "No."

"In fact," she continued, trying to imbue her voice with more confidence than she felt, "I can imagine there could be benefits to letting the staff—as well as Theo's business colleagues—think he's still alive."

The pause was longer this time, and she was afraid she had overplayed her hand.

Eventually, Lucas said, "There *are* some people who could make our lives unpleasant if they knew Herr Viklund was dead."

Lucas being willing to overlook the likelihood that Louise

had poisoned his late employer was good; Lucas throwing in his lot as a co-conspirator was even better.

"Exactly," she said. "We mustn't rush into any decisions. It's a sensitive situation and we need to plan how to handle it carefully. Is there a part of the compound where we could claim Theo was staying and be assured that none of the staff would discover otherwise?"

"His suite," said Maja promptly. "No one on the house-keeping staff goes there, other than me." She looked at Lucas.

"No one on the security staff would go into Herr Viklund's suite without specific instructions from me," he said. "But it's possible someone saw him come from the main house to the lab—they tend to stay informed of his location, if only to stay out of his way. They'll wonder how he came to be in his quarters."

"Perhaps you and Maja could be seen escorting someone resembling Theo to his suite."

"And who would that be?" Lucas asked, but his eyes were already sliding toward Edmund.

Edmund's eyebrows shot up. "You want me to pretend to be Viklund?"

"You're about the same height," said Louise, "and a similar build. We can cut your hair short, and dress you in his clothes."

Edmund glanced at the body. "Which clothes?"

"The simplest thing is for you to wear the suit he was wearing when he came to the lab."

"Can't Maja bring me one of his suits from the house?"

"Let's keep things simple, Edmund," she said, not entirely hiding her irritation.

"There's that hair clipper in your apartment, Doctor Rinnert," said Maja. "From when you first got here."

"Perfect," said Louise, not waiting for the inevitable

complaint from Edmund. "And, Maja and Lucas, if you can clear the way between the lab and Theo's suite, no one will see Edmund up close."

"Yes," said Lucas, "that might work. And it wouldn't be so unusual. Viklund didn't like to encounter staff when he walked through the house or on the grounds."

"Of course, we'll need to explain why Edmund isn't in the lab—" said Louise.

Edmund snorted derisively. "You think anyone other than these two would notice? My exposure to Viklund's staff is pretty limited." After a moment, he added, his voice hard, "My exposure to anywhere other than the lab is pretty limited."

Louise suppressed a sigh. Her plan to eliminate Theo had gone as smoothly as she could have hoped, at least so far. She didn't need the added distraction of Edmund's resentment that he hadn't been on Theo's guest A-list.

"We need a reason Theo would stay out of sight of the staff." She cast her gaze upward and let a quarter of a minute tick by. The longer the conversation continued, the more certain she was that neither Lucas nor Maja actually believed that Theo's death had been accidental. However, there was no harm in pretending she hadn't been constructing her plan for days. "I know Theo and Rey were close—more like father and daughter than uncle and niece—so we could say that Theo learned something about Rey's death, something so upsetting that it sent him into a tailspin, and he had to go into seclusion to process it."

"He *was* very upset by her death," said Maja.

"And what might he have learned that would drive him into seclusion?" asked Lucas.

"Something so terrible that he couldn't bring himself to discuss it," said Louise, "even with the two of you. And who else would he tell?" The question was both rhetorical and actual.

"No one on the staff, certainly," said Lucas. "And other than staff, there is no one else at the compound except you and Doctor Rinnert."

Edmund snorted. "And he would only talk to me when I happened to be in the lab when he visited Louise."

"Edmund," Louise said curtly, "it's not a popularity contest."

He stuffed his hands in his pockets and glowered at her.

"So we have a plan to get Doctor Rinnert into Herr Viklund's suite," said Lucas, "and an explanation for why he's there. But how long can we maintain that story?"

"It seems plausible that Theo might retire to his suite for at least several days—perhaps longer—in the face of devastating information about his niece's death," said Louise. "What would we need to do to make his presence in his quarters plausible?"

"I can bring in meals," said Maja.

"I'm gratified you're going to let me eat," muttered Edmund.

"And I can visit his suite as well," said Lucas. "Viklund would want to continue to get his normal security updates from me."

Louise couldn't have asked for a better set-up for the suggestion she was sure would seal Lucas's commitment to her plan. "You could tell the staff that Theo had designated you as second-in-command."

To her surprise, Lucas for the first time seemed uncomfortable. "No, I don't think so. It would seem ..." He waved his hand, as if to summon the word he was searching for. "... thinking only of myself ..."

"Self-serving?" she suggested.

"Yes, self-serving. I think it's best if we claim you're Viklund's second."

Louise glanced at Maja, whose attitude toward this suggestion was impossible to read in her stoic expression, and Edmund, whose scowl made his attitude only too easy to read. She tamped down her growing anger with him. He should be happy to be alive, not angry about forfeiting the figurehead position to Louise. She turned back to Lucas. "Very well. If you think that's best."

Louise herself as Theo Viklund's second-in-command?

This situation might work out even better than she had hoped.

2

L ouise briefly considered suggesting that the four of them sit at the lab table, then rejected the idea. She didn't want to undermine the role Lucas was recommending she play by implying that she thought of the four of them as equals. She could hardly invite Lucas but not Maja to join her at the table, and although she would have been all too happy to exclude Edmund from the invitation, she doubted he would cooperate. She remained standing.

"How many people will we need to convince that Theo is in his quarters?" she asked. "Let's start with the staff. Who did Theo interact with?"

"Mainly me and Maja," said Lucas. "The girl who helps serve at meals. The cook. Elsa."

Louise remembered Elsa, a pretty young woman who wouldn't have looked out of place gracing the cover of a fashion magazine. Someone who didn't know Theo as well as Louise had come to know him might assume Elsa was at the compound for his entertainment or possibly the entertainment of his guests. But Louise suspected that Theo had thought of Elsa much as he thought of the spaces in the house he decorated to match the preferences of his guests: as a piece of attractive décor.

"That's it?" Louise asked. "It must take a large staff to maintain the house, not to mention the security staff."

"He would never see most of the household staff," said Maja, "like the girls who do the laundry or clean the rooms."

"I see people working on the grounds," ventured Edmund.

"If Herr Viklund wanted to go outside," said Maja, "we would make sure there was no one nearby."

"It's helpful that the number of people Theo interacted with at the compound is small," said Louise. "But even those who didn't encounter him directly will eventually wonder what's going on if he goes into his suite and doesn't come out. Can we reduce the size of the staff to reduce the risk?"

"Sending some of the staff away would have benefits," said Lucas, "but I don't want to sacrifice security for our convenience."

"And a house this big requires many people to maintain it to an acceptable level," said Maja.

"Perhaps we could bring in new people," said Louise. "People who have no previous exposure to Theo and so don't know what is and isn't odd about the current situation." She didn't add that almost everything about the life Theo had created at the compound was odd.

"Perhaps," said Lucas. "But the process of finding candidates and then doing the necessary background checks could take weeks, maybe months."

"The two of you should determine how small a staff you could get by with for a few months." She smiled at Maja. "And during that time, we can adjust our expectations of what an acceptable level is."

"Maja and I will discuss this," said Lucas, "and decide who should stay and who can be sent back to Sweden."

"They won't spread rumors when they get home?" asked Edmund, skeptical.

Lucas raised an eyebrow. "Not if they know what's good for them. And their families."

Deciding that she didn't need to know exactly what Lucas meant by that—at least not at the moment—Louise said, "Speaking of family, am I right in assuming that, with Rey gone, there are no relatives of Theo's that we need to worry about?"

"Actually," said Maja, "I have heard Herr Viklund talking to his brother—Rey's father, Karl—on the phone."

Louise scowled. She should have factored Rey's father into her calculations. "Were Karl and Theo close?"

"Not very close, but with Rey's death ..." Maja shrugged. "I think Herr Karl was asking Herr Viklund for information about what happened to Rey, and Herr Viklund kept telling him he had no information."

Louise turned her wedding ring on her finger, then stopped herself—it was a distracting habit she was trying to break. "We'll cross that bridge when we come to it. We also need to consider who Theo interacted with outside the compound. How about business colleagues?"

"Herr Viklund hasn't left the compound in several years," said Lucas. "He conducts any business on the computer in his suite."

"We need to get into that computer," said Louise. "We need to see who he was corresponding with, and if anyone is waiting for a response from him."

"He unlocked the computer by putting his hand on a plate—"

"Biometric authentication," said Louise. "Can you bring his computer to the lab?"

"No, it's not small, like a laptop. And the plate is attached to the desk—it might not work if I removed it. Or if we moved the desk."

"So we need to bring Theo to the computer."

"Not necessarily all of him," said Edmund, not entirely hiding his enthusiasm. "Just his hand."

Louise tried to avoid glancing down at Edmund's thumbless left hand, thinking back with a shudder to the calm tone Theo has used when he described what had happened to it: *I don't want you to think we're barbarians. We didn't hack off his thumb like some gang of Italian mafiosi. No, it was all very civilized —a simple operation in our little dispensary. He was completely anesthetized the entire time.*

Theo had claimed that he had taken Edmund's left thumb because he believed—erroneously, as it turned out—that Edmund was right-handed.

Louise suspected that if Theo's hand needed to be separated from his body, Edmund would be only too happy to perform the procedure, but she didn't intend to cater to Edmund's morbid whims. "I'll remove the hand while you change into Theo's clothes, Edmund." She turned to Lucas. "Which hand did he use to unlock the computer?"

"Left."

Louise looked down at Theo's body. "We need to decide the best method of removal ..."

"There are scalpels in the dispensary," said Lucas.

She shot him a look. "I'm well aware." Returning her gaze to the body, she continued. "Those will be useful, but we may need to cut through bone as well. Is there a bone saw?"

"I don't know about a bone saw." After a moment, Lucas added, "There are branch cutters in the gardener's shed."

"No," said Edmund. "We should make as clean a cut as possible. A crushing amputation might distort the palm print."

"Excellent point, Edmund," said Louise, relieved he was finally taking a productive role in the conversation.

"I'll see what I can find in the dispensary," said Lucas. "And while I'm at the house, I'll tell the staff to stay out of the way of the path Herr Viklund will take back to his suite."

As Lucas stepped outside, Louise turned to Edmund and Maja, "We need to get Theo's clothes off."

The two women struggled with Theo's uncooperative corpse and Edmund offered unhelpful suggestions until Louise told him to keep an eye out the door to make sure that no one other than Lucas came up the path from the house.

They removed Theo's shoes, socks, suit, tie, and shirt. In the pocket of the pants, Louise found a phone. Perhaps, she thought, it wouldn't be necessary to access Theo's computer after all. Pressing his finger to the biometric sensor unlocked the phone, but the home screen was oddly devoid of apps other than the defaults. The Contacts app contained no contacts, the Email app no email, the Phone app no record of previous calls or voicemails. There was a browser icon, but now was hardly the time to catch up on the news to which she had been denied access during her weeks at the compound. She put the phone next to the lab computer, one that provided access to the confidential data of dozens of renown medical and research institutions but none to any public internet sites.

As Maja was brushing dust from Theo's jacket, Edmund turned from the open door. "Lucas is coming back."

Lucas entered, carrying a canvas tote bag. He transferred its contents onto the lab table: an assortment of scalpels and, to Louise's surprise, a Satterlee bone saw. She pushed away thoughts of the circumstances in which a bone saw might have been put to use in Theo's dispensary.

"We need to get him on the table," she said. "But do we

have anything we can cover the table with? Plastic sheeting? A tarp?"

"Those would be in the workshop in the house or in the gardener's shed," said Lucas with some irritation, "but it's going to look suspicious if we keep running out to bring supplies back to the lab."

"We could use a bedspread to cover the table," said Maja.

Louise didn't see how Maja bringing a bedspread back from the house was any less suspicious than Lucas bringing a tarp from the gardener's shed, but Lucas didn't seem to object.

"Yes, let's do that," said Louise.

However, instead of going to the door that led to the path to the house, Maja crossed the lab and disappeared through the door leading to Edmund's quarters. Louise wondered if Edmund would object to his bedspread being used to wrap the body of the man he had helped kill, but he appeared unconcerned.

Maja returned a moment later with a spread in a geometric pattern of purple and green. It was not a design Louise would have imagined Edmund choosing, although the combination of amethyst and emerald was one Louise herself found especially pleasing. Perhaps Maja had chosen the décor for his accommodations.

When they covered the table with the bedspread, it hung off one side and bunched on the floor.

"It's too much cloth," said Louise. "He's not going to bleed a great deal, but there will be some fluid, and I don't want to be dealing with more stained cloth than is necessary. Let's cut off the excess."

She found a pair of scissors in a drawer in one of the lab's workstations, and Maja cut away half the spread, then folded the remnant and set it aside.

Then they—mainly Lucas and Maja—lifted Theo's body onto the lab table.

"Edmund," said Louise, "why don't you get changed, and Maja can help you with the haircut."

Maja followed a sullen Edmund through the door at the back of the lab that led to his quarters.

Louise picked up Theo's phone and was about to put it in her pocket, but Lucas held out his hand.

"I should keep that for now," he said.

"But why? If I'm to be announced as Theo's second-in-command—"

"While I was looking for the supplies you needed, I thought of something else. As far as I know, most of the staff have no reason to think you are anything but a guest of Herr Viklund. But Anders knows you tried to escape, and that you were brought back against your will."

"Who is Anders?"

Lucas's face remained expressionless. "He was the other person in the truck."

Louise had gotten as far as the road, her feet nearly frozen, her nerves nearly shot, when she had seen the *AJ's Plumbing* truck parked on the shoulder. The driver had signaled to her that he was deaf and mute, but Louise should have known it was a ploy to prevent him from revealing the Swedish accent he shared with all of Theo's staff. She had not been entirely surprised when Lucas had appeared from the back of the truck, and the two men had driven her back to the compound to face Theo.

Trying to keep her expression neutral, she asked, "And what are we going to do about that?"

"Anders is not well liked. If we let word slip out that he has committed a ..." He groped for the word.

"Transgression?"

"Yes, a transgression. No one would be too surprised—or sorry—if he disappeared." He was silent for a few moments, then continued. "Actually, we could imply that Anders played a role in Rey's death, and that the cause of Herr Viklund's distress is the knowledge that a member of his staff killed his niece."

"Yes, that is good." After a pause, she asked, "And what would the expected penalty for such a transgression be?"

Lucas drew a casual finger across his throat. "I'll take care of Anders," he said, "but while he's still around, we can't risk pretending that Herr Viklund has invited you to his suite." He nodded toward the phone. "And we can't have you answering his phone."

Louise was about to point out that her having it didn't mean she had to answer it, but it didn't seem worth an argument. She handed the phone to Lucas. "When will Anders be out of the way?"

"If we use the story that Herr Viklund has gone into seclusion because of a revelation about Anders' involvement in Rey's death, then it makes sense that he would be taken care of immediately. I'll do it tonight."

Louise nodded. "Very good." She donned nitrile gloves, arranged Theo's arm at the corner of the lab table, and set to work.

She applied makeshift tourniquets above and below where she would cut, a few inches above the wrist. That would not only contain any fluid but also, she hoped, help retain the shape of the hand and preserve the viability of the palm print as long as possible.

Once she had used the scalpel to cut through the skin, muscles, and tendons, Lucas also pulled on gloves and held the arm in place while Louise sawed. When the hand was detached, she wrapped it in a piece of plastic wrap and put it in the lab's refrigeration unit.

"What do we do with the rest of him?" asked Lucas.

"If bringing a tarp from the gardener's shed would have raised eyebrows, we can't very well drag him into the woods and bury him." She gestured to a large chest freezer in the corner of the lab. "We can put him in there, at least for now."

The freezer had been added to the lab's complement of equipment a few days earlier, after Louise told Theo she needed it to store a rotating supply of the lab's sequencer and flow cytometry reagents.

If Lucas noted the coincidence of timing, he didn't comment.

Louise lifted the freezer's lid, and a wisp of cooled air curled out over the lip of the compartment. Then, with Lucas at Theo's head and Louise at his feet, they grasped the corners of the bedspread and hoisted the body into the freezer, setting the fog of cold air swirling and then settling over the body.

She and Lucas peeled off their gloves and dropped them in the biohazard bin, and Lucas shrugged his sport coat back into place on his shoulders.

"Can we get a lock put on the freezer?" she asked, pushing a strand of hair away from her face with the back of her hand.

"There's no need," said Lucas. "No one on the staff will come into the lab without instructions from me or Maja."

She hesitated. As circumstances had proven, there was plenty going on in the lab that Lucas was unaware of—he hadn't known of Theo's collapse until Louise had summoned him—but it didn't seem worth pressing. "Very well." She glanced toward the closed door to Edmund's quarters. Lowering her voice, she said, "Doctor Rinnert bears watching."

"Yes."

"He'll be in Theo's suite alone, at least some of the time—it seems unrealistic for you or Maja to stay with him all the time. Is there anything in the suite that would give him information we don't want him to have?"

"Not without the ability to access the computer."

She nodded. "We need to figure out how to get the hand into Theo's suite."

Lucas considered for a moment, then said, clearly trying to suppress a smile, "Maja will need to bring in meals—she could bring the hand in under one of the plate covers."

Louise startled herself with a snort of laughter, and the more she tried to get it under control, the more it slipped away from her. Normally she wasn't one to succumb to inappropriate—or even appropriate—bursts of merriment, but the circumstances were hardly normal. Although embarrassing, she supposed this reaction to the stress of the situation was less damaging that others she could imagine.

Half a minute later, when she heard the click of the door to Edmund's suite open, she was blotting her eyes with a tissue and Lucas was no longer bothering to hide his amusement.

Edmund stepped into the lab, followed by Maja.

No one would mistake Edmund Rinnert for Theo Viklund up close, but if Lucas and Maja could ensure the path between the lab and Theo's suite was clear, proximity wouldn't be an issue. The suit was a reasonably good fit, and Edmund's previously shaggy hair, which Louise had thought of as brown, looked in its new crewcut style closer to Theo's steel gray.

"Having fun?" asked Edmund. His voice was a sneer, but Louise sensed an undercurrent of something else. Resentment? Fear? What would he assume about her uncharacteristic behavior?

She tamped down the last hiccup of laughter. "Not particularly." She cleared her throat. "I'd say that with the clothes and the new haircut, you'll be a convincing Theo."

"The shoes are too small," said Edmund.

"If Theo is sufficiently upset by whatever he learned about Rey's death to go into seclusion, he would no doubt be unsteady on his feet. We can use that to explain any difficulty you have walking." She hurried on before Edmund could lodge another complaint. "Lucas and Maja, you escort Edmund back to the main house. I'll finish straightening up here, then go back to my suite."

Lucas and Maja nodded their assent, and they and Edmund went to the door that led outside. Maja positioned herself next to Edmund and took his arm: a faithful employee tending to her distraught employer. Lucas opened the door and stood back to let the pair pass, then followed them out.

Louise went to the door and watched the three make their way toward the main house, Lucas and Maja supporting an evidently prostrate Theo Viklund between them.

When they disappeared from sight, Louise let out a long, trembling breath. Her plan was proceeding as smoothly as she could have hoped. In fact, it was proceeding even more smoothly, since Lucas appeared willing to turn the reins over to her, at least in terms of how he and Maja presented Louise's role to the staff. But there was nothing preventing Edmund Rinnert from trying to talk Lucas and Maja into joining forces against Louise. For that matter, there was nothing preventing him from calling out to household or security staff that he was not, in fact, Theo Viklund, but the scientist who had been sequestered in the lab for the last three years. Nothing other than Lucas and Maja, who at least now had as much incentive as she did to hide what had happened in the lab.

Theo had lured Edmund to the compound with the promise of protecting him from prosecution for falsifying research results, but Edmund's scientific work at the compound had failed to provide the value Theo expected. When Theo heard that his long-time colleague Louise Mortensen was fending off unwanted scrutiny into her medical experiments by the state attorney general, he had used the same ploy on her. Edmund had been demoted to serve as her lab assistant, but Louise had become just as much a prisoner at the compound as he was. The difference was that she had been prepared to do something about it.

She sighed. She couldn't monitor Edmund every minute. His lack of initiative had played into her plan so far. She hoped he didn't choose now to turn over a new leaf.

She turned and scanned the lab. The pieces of Theo's teacup still lay on the floor, and Louise collected them and dropped them into the biohazard bin. Now the only evidence of what had transpired was the half of the bedspread Maja had cut away, lying folded on the table. Louise picked up the remnant and crossed to the door through which Maja had accompanied Edmund to help him don his disguise.

Louise had never entered Edmund's quarters, and she found herself in a small vestibule off of which two doors opened. She opened the one on the left and stepped into a room that looked like a cross between a rudimentary dorm room and a well-appointed prison cell. The tops of the wooden dresser and desk were bare. A starkly functional armoire stood in for a built-in closet. Along one wall was a kitchenette: sink, two-burner stove, microwave. The door of the under-the-counter refrigerator was slightly ajar. The bed was bare, except for a pile of green-and-purple patterned sheets piled neatly at its center.

She backed out of the room, closed the door, and opened the one on the right.

This room was identical in furnishings and lay-out but was

obviously inhabited. Boxes of breakfast cereals stood on the narrow kitchenette counter. A spine-sprung paperback lay on the bedside table next to a half-full glass of water and a bottle of NyQuil. The bedspread, a bright red, was rumpled, and the clothes Edmund had been wearing were tossed on top of it.

She backed out of the apartment and closed the door. Then, heart thumping, she turned back to the door opposite Edmund's and opened it again. The sheets on the bed matched the remnant she held, and now she realized what the color scheme had reminded her of. It was the same as that of the large geometric painting that hung over the gas fireplace in her suite in the main house.

Edmund had certainly not arrived at Theo's compound with his own bedspread, and Maja must have provided him with a bedspread she thought would provide a spot of color in his otherwise bleak space.

Had Maja done the same for a room that was intended for Louise?

When Louise had planned Theo's murder, she had thought she was escaping life as a prisoner in her elegantly appointed suite. She had never imagined that she might have to trade her suite for this unprepossessing space.

She had visited Theo Viklund at his compound a dozen times over the previous decade, and she had believed him to consider her, if not a friend, at least a respected colleague. But his veneer of civility had finally been stripped away when he had laid out the quid pro quo for keeping Louise out of the hands of the authorities: he expected her to apply her medical knowledge in support of whatever nefarious plan held his attention at the moment. She had become nothing but a subject matter expert to him, one whose expertise he was willing to extract under duress. If she had needed more justification for killing Theo—which she did not—this glimpse into what her future would have been like as Theo's captive provided it.

She drew herself up even more erect that her normally ramrod-straight posture, placed the remnant on top of the bed, and returned to the lab.

With one last scan of the room, she slipped into her coat, then stepped outside and started down the path toward the house.

Theo's body was relegated to a freezer, Lucas and Maja had provisionally thrown their support behind her, and Edmund was at least temporarily out of the way. She might not be able to occupy Theo's suite—Edmund would be staying there, at least for now—but at least she would retain her own comfortable quarters in the main house.

More importantly, Louise would occupy Theo's life. Her initial goal had been to escape from the compound, and to do so in such a way that she didn't blunder into the grasp of the authorities and land in a prison even more unpleasant than the bare room in the lab annex. But if she could access the information she needed from Theo's computer, there was no reason she couldn't convince not only his staff but also his colleagues that he was alive and well. How would they ever find out that the wizard behind the curtain was no longer Theo Viklund but Louise Mortensen?

ROOK TAKES BISHOP

3

L ouise stood at the floor-to-ceiling windows of her suite, looking out at the woods surrounding the house, the trees' branches gradually merging into one undifferentiated mass in the growing darkness.

Half an hour before, Elsa had delivered Louise's dinner and laid it out on the dining table. Elsa wasn't her usual graceful self—as she was laying out the silverware, she dropped the heavy sterling knife onto the bread plate with a nerve-jarring clatter. Louise waved away Elsa's almost tearful apology and the young woman hurried out of the suite. Louise didn't chalk up Elsa's demeanor to upset over a mishandled utensil; if Lucas planned to make an example of Anders, word was no doubt already circulating among the staff.

Louise hadn't even bothered to remove the plates' silver domed covers. She had nearly convinced herself that her lack of appetite was due to the stress of the day, not an irrational dread that one of the plates might hold an amputated hand.

In fact, the space she had previously thought of as her sanctuary within Theo's compound held little appeal for her now. For example, she would never again enjoy the painting hanging over the gas fireplace. When she had first come to the compound, the pop of color its amethyst and emerald elements provided in the otherwise soothing ivory, creams, and grays of the rest of the room had pleased her. No more.

She thought with embarrassment about how closely Theo had managed to match her subconscious preferences for décor. Since he apparently decorated the guest rooms to match his guests' tastes, one might have expected that he would have matched the décor of Louise's former Pocopson home. But that house had been decorated to her late husband Gerard's tastes, not her own. She had never minded—home décor was low on her list of priorities—but the appearance of the suite had satisfied her in a way her own home never had.

And as she thought back to the purple and green linens neatly stacked in the bleak room in the lab annex, she felt something near shame that Theo Viklund had duped her so thoroughly about what his long-term plans for her were.

When she had first arrived at the compound, the prospect of being able to pursue her research in the well-appointed lab Theo provided had its attractions. It was certainly better than waiting for the police or representatives of the Pennsylvania attorney general's office to arrive at her home with awkward questions—or an arrest warrant.

She and Gerard had become too cavalier about the need to maintain secrecy around their work at the Vivantem fertility clinic. When the babies of their test subjects—their *patients*, she corrected herself—began displaying indications of special abilities, she had been happy to monitor developments from afar. But once those babies grew into adults, the possibilities had become so much more intriguing. Fatally intriguing, at least for Gerard. And inconveniently attention-getting for the police and the AG's office.

Theo had assured her he had had those investigations

terminated—but had he really? And even if he had, she could hardly return to a quiet life of research and study if she left the compound. Staying here was her best option in the short term. And, if she were to take on Theo's role, perhaps the best option in the long term as well. She might wish for another cohort of subjects—*patients*—whose off-spring's powers might prove useful in her current situation, but a new generation of genetically modified babies wouldn't bear fruit for many years. What she needed was a contingent of specially equipped allies right now.

She heard a knock on the door and called, "Come in!"

Lucas stepped in, and Louise was unsurprised that she couldn't glean any sense of the status of their situation from his demeanor. He would probably look the same if he was delivering the evening paper as if he was preparing to execute a death sentence. A valuable characteristic in an ally. A disconcerting characteristic in an enemy.

"Doctor Rinnert is settled in the suite," he said. "We have no reason to think that any of the staff suspects it's not Viklund."

"Is Edmund there alone?"

"No. Maja is with him."

"We need to make sure he can't contact anyone."

"He won't be able to. He has no phone. Speaking of which —" He drew a phone from his pocket. "—a call came in on Viklund's phone from his brother. Herr Karl left a voicemail message, but I can't open the phone without accessing Viklund's body, and under normal circumstances, I never go to the lab unless you're there." He allowed himself a small smile. "We might need to remove his right index finger as well."

Louise grimaced. "Hardly necessary. We could go to the lab now—"

"No. I'm going to be a bit busy this evening. I recommend you keep the phone and, if Karl calls back, give him the story about Viklund going into seclusion and you taking over as his second."

"If Karl doubts our story about my new role, it sounds as if Anders is the only person on the staff who could refute our claim. Is there any way Karl could get in touch with him?"

"It would be unlikely—Viklund didn't encourage guests to fraternize with the staff—but very shortly we won't have to worry about anyone talking with Anders."

"Very well." She took the phone from Lucas and slipped it into her pocket. "Is there anything you can tell me about Karl? Anything that would make the conversation go more smoothly?"

Lucas shook his head. "Maja might know more, but I doubt it. Herr Karl hasn't been to the compound for many years, and she would have had no reason to chat with him when he was here."

She nodded. "I'll try to keep the conversation with Karl as generic as possible."

"If there's nothing else ..." he said, turning to leave.

"Lucas, I'd like a phone of my own. One that I can use to access the internet. I'd like to be able to catch up on the news, even just to check the weather before I leave the house to walk to the lab." The phone Theo had given her worked only to contact compound staff.

"Certainly. I'll have Elsa bring you one."

"Thank you." She raised a hand before he could turn away again. "And I know you have a lot to take care of, but I want to take one more minute of your time."

He glanced at his watch, then sighed. "Very well."

"We'll be more likely to meet both our goals if we are open with each other about what they are. I believe you know what mine are: not to live as a prisoner, and not to fall into the hands of people who would want to prosecute me for actions they think I took before I came to the compound. I also hope to continue to do research and other scientific work, and to do it in a reasonably comfortable environment." Her voice grew frosty. "Not, for example, in the apartment off the lab that Theo had evidently intended as my long-term residence."

She watched for a reaction from Lucas, but his expression remained unreadable.

"And are you willing to tell me what your goals are?" she asked.

After a pause, he said, "More money would be helpful. I send money to my family in Sweden."

"If we can access Theo's computer, I hope we will be able to access his bank accounts as well, and I'll make sure you and Maja are amply rewarded for your ..." She stopped. She had been about to say *assistance*, but she suspected Lucas wouldn't appreciate being framed as an assistant. "... roles in our plan. So more money would satisfy your goals?"

"Money provides power, and power paves the way to other goals. Like you, I would prefer not to be answerable to another person."

She was glad for her discretion in her choice of words. "I hope you don't think that I consider you answerable to me."

He raised an eyebrow. "Considering the situation, we need to be answerable to each other. At least for now."

"And do you include Edmund in that assessment?"

"I don't consider myself answerable to Doctor Rinnert, but he has his uses."

"At least for now?" asked Louise, echoing Lucas's qualification.

His answering smile was predatory. "Exactly."

"And Maja?"

His features resumed their normal inscrutable expression. "We must ensure Maja is rewarded for her help, but I don't think she minds taking a supporting role, as long as she is treated fairly."

"So, you and I, then ..."

"... are partners, as long as need be. We both bring useful expertise and can both benefit from the other's expertise."

"I agree." After a pause, she asked, "And you agree to continue to let the staff—and others outside the compound—think Theo is living in seclusion in his suite?" She was still curious, and a bit mistrustful, about Lucas's willingness to go along with the charade.

"I have reasons for wanting others to believe that Herr Viklund is still alive."

"And what are those reasons?"

He cocked an eyebrow at her.

"Lucas, we can best help each other if we lay all our cards on the table."

She thought he was going to refuse to answer, but then he shrugged. "Some of the things I have done for Herr Viklund have earned me enemies. But his position and his reputation have provided me with some protection. My enemies know he would avenge any harm done to me. If they know he's dead, they would be quick to act."

"Then we will do our best to ensure that they don't know that."

Lucas glanced at this watch. "I'll go now. The sooner Anders is out of the way, the better."

"I agree. Thank you for taking care of him."

The wolfish smile returned. "It will be my pleasure."

Lucas left, and a few minutes later, a still-flustered Elsa arrived at Louise's suite with a phone. Louise considered passing the time by using it to find out what had been going on in the world since she had arrived at the compound weeks ago. However, not only couldn't she see how anything happening outside the compound could bear on her immediate situation, but she was too distracted by the idea of how the Anders situation was progressing.

Less than an hour later, Louise was once again standing by the windows when she saw the beams of two flashlights moving through the trees, headed away from the house. She watched the lights until they disappeared behind one of the hills that rolled across the property.

To keep her mind off what she suspected was going to happen—or was now happening—in the woods, she considered how she would identify herself to Karl Viklund if he called.

If Karl already knew her identity, she'd decide how to deal with that situation when it arose. But she guessed Theo wouldn't have shared the story of his fugitive guest with his brother, and if Karl didn't already know her identity, she wasn't about to provide it.

At the same time, identifying herself only as *Louise* made her sound like an underling, and she was more likely to convince Karl of whatever she needed to convince him of if he believed she was in fact Theo's trusted second-in-command.

She almost yelped when Theo's phone rang. She pulled it out of her pocket and read the caller ID: *Karl.*

She tapped *Accept.* "This is Theo Viklund's phone. I believe this is Theo's brother, Karl?"

There was a pause, then a voice that sounded very much like Theo's, lightly accented with Swedish, said, "Yes, this is Karl. Who is this? And where is Theo?"

"My name is Louise Gerard, and I want to start out by saying how sorry I was to hear about your daughter Rey's death."

"You know about that?"

"Yes. I've been Theo's guest here at the compound, and he let me know."

"You're a *friend* of Theo's?" Karl's disbelief that his brother would have a *friend* was clear.

"I wouldn't presume to call myself a friend, but Theo and I are colleagues, and he invited me here to do some research."

"You're doing research with Theo?"

"Not *with* him—*for* him. I'd prefer you hear about it from your brother. But," she hurried on, "I'm afraid that can't happen right now. Theo was quite distraught when Rey died, and then earlier today he got some information about Rey's death that further upset him."

Karl's voice spiked. "What information?"

"I don't know. All I know is that he retreated to his suite and said he will see no one."

"No one at all?"

"The housekeeper, Maja, brings him meals, and he consults with Lucas, his head of security."

"How about you?"

Louise's gaze drifted toward the windows. "I expect to be able to speak with Theo tomorrow."

"And he specifically said he didn't want to talk to me?"

"Not you specifically. If he didn't need to keep things running smoothly at the compound—and didn't have to eat— he probably wouldn't even see Lucas and Maja."

Louise winced at a muffled sound from outside that she thought might be a gunshot.

"Karl, I apologize—I have to go. An experiment I'm running needs my attention. But I'll encourage Theo to call you as soon as possible."

She ended the call and peered into the darkness, which was now absolute.

An hour later, she saw light moving back toward the house.

Now it was a single beam.

~

AS MIDNIGHT NEARED, Louise was still on her feet but practically swaying with exhaustion. She didn't want to sit down, afraid she'd fall asleep. She wanted to be awake if Lucas came with a report, but she also knew her sleep would be troubled by visions of the consequences if the staff saw through their plan, or if Lucas rethought the wisdom of their partnership.

She jumped at a light knock on the suite door. She drew a calming breath, then called, "Come in!"

Lucas stepped in. His hair was damp, as if he had showered. Rather than his usual slacks, white shirt, and sport coat, he was wearing a fleece and jeans.

"Anders is no longer an issue," he said.

"I heard what sounded like a gunshot."

"Yes."

"If I heard it, others might have heard it as well."

"But we wanted the others to hear it—no? To understand what happens to those who cross Herr Viklund ..." He raised an eyebrow. "... or cross those who are carrying out his orders."

"Good point. But what about people outside the property? Might a neighbor have heard it?"

"There are no neighbors."

"Very good." After a beat, she added, "Thank you for taking care of that."

He gave her a quick nod.

"I assume Anders is—" She gestured toward the window.

"Yes." He smiled. "He was even obliging enough to dig his own grave."

She raised an eyebrow. "Convenient. And is there any possibility of someone finding the grave?"

"No."

"Hikers exploring the grounds?" she pressed.

He clasped his hands behind his back—a military *at ease*. "The grounds are fenced."

"Someone could climb the fences."

"No one climbs the fences without my knowledge." After a beat, he added, "And no one crawls under them without my knowledge. As you well know."

Louise willed herself not to look away from Lucas's gaze. "Yes," she said coldly, "I know from personal experience how effective Theo's security was."

"It wasn't Viklund's security. It's *my* security."

"I didn't mean to imply otherwise."

"If our partnership is to work, you must let me take care of those parts of our plan that are *my* areas of expertise, just as I must let you take care of those parts that are *your* area of expertise."

"Of course."

His eyes stayed on her for a moment, then he turned and left the suite.

Louise pulled one of the dining chairs away from the table and sank onto it.

Lucas had called their relationship a partnership, and she would do well not to forget that.

QUEEN FORK

In queen fork, the queen attacks the opponent's bishop, forcing the opponent to choose which piece to save.

Endgame Essentials: Navigating to Checkmate by Will Fielding

4

As it happened, the hand did make it into Theo's suite with a meal delivery, although not on a covered plate. Louise packed it carefully in an insulated bag, which Maja then placed, under a tablecloth, on the bottom shelf of the serving trolley.

Louise and Lucas followed Maja and the trolley down the center hallway of the house. Some distance past the formal dining room, where Theo had entertained Louise during her earliest visits, the hall narrowed and began a gradual downward slope. Recessed fixtures cast a soft, shadowless light. The floor's cork tiles muffled their steps, the only sounds the rattle of the dishes on the trolley and the barely audible whoosh of circulating air.

As they continued to walk, Louise tried to calculate where they were in relation to the other parts of the complex with which she was familiar. They must be beyond the outer walls of the main house, under the forested ground she viewed from her window.

"His suite is underground?" she asked Lucas, her voice barely more than a whisper.

"Yes. Some of the staff call Herr Viklund's quarters 'the bunker.'"

The corridor turned, and immediately ahead of them was a door, next to which sat one of Theo's blond-haired, blue-eyed staffers—a man Louise recalled seeing around the compound but whose name she didn't know. The sounds of the trolley would have alerted him to their approach, but she noticed there was also an angled mirror that gave him a view down the corridor.

"Emil," said Lucas, "this is Doctor Mortensen. Herr Viklund has given approval for her to enter his suite."

Emil examined Louise expressionlessly and nodded.

Maja knocked lightly on the door—Louise hoped Edmund was smart enough not to call *Come in!* in a voice that was obviously not Theo Viklund's—then opened the door and stepped inside. Louise and Lucas followed.

Louise had been curious to see Theo's suite. Considering how expansive and comfortable her own suite in the main house was, she expected his to be even more opulent. But it more closely resembled the featureless apartment off the lab, although on a larger scale.

The living area was a single large room, with a door she guessed led to the bedroom and bathroom. Straight ahead was a dining area with a Danish modern table and single chair. Through a door beyond the table, she could see a sparely equipped galley kitchen. On the left was exercise equipment: a treadmill, a rower, and a strength machine.

On the right was an enormous desk, also Danish modern, on which stood a computer monitor and keyboard. Beyond that was a conference table, its one chair facing a compact but professional-looking video set-up complete with boom mic and ring lights. Serving as the background of the videoconference set-up was a rug in a bright Middle Eastern pattern that hung on the wall and a potted plant illuminated from off-screen by a grow light mounted on a stand. No virtual backgrounds for Theo Viklund.

Other than the background decor of the videoconference area, the room was devoid of color. Not a picture hung on the walls, not a pillow graced the furniture. In fact, she realized, other than the straight-back chairs at the desk, the conference table, and the dining table, there was nowhere to sit. No couch. No upholstered easy chairs. The lack of windows added a sense of claustrophobia.

If Theo Viklund had taken such care to decorate his guests' accommodations to match their personalities, what did this space, devoid of any grace notes or embellishments, mean about his own personality? A bunker, indeed.

"Do we need to re-lock the door?" she whispered.

"The door is soundproof," said Lucas, his voice a normal volume, "and Emil knows better than to come in."

Maja began transferring the covered dishes from the trolley to the dining table.

"Where is Edmund?" asked Louise.

Her question was answered by the flush of a toilet in the adjoining room and the sound of water running in a sink. A moment later, Edmund appeared, wearing new-looking jeans and a sweatshirt. She couldn't imagine Theo in jeans and a sweatshirt—Maja must have smuggled some alternative clothes into the suite for Edmund.

"Hello, Edmund," she greeted him. "How are you enjoying your new quarters?"

"Did you know they call this place 'the bunker'?" he asked peevishly.

"So I hear," she said sourly. Evidently a more expansive, if not cheerier, space had not improved Edmund's mood. She nodded toward the table. "Would you like to have your breakfast before we get started?"

"No—I'm not hungry."

"Very well." She turned to Maja. "That will be all, Maja. Thank you."

Maja cast her eye across the plates on the dining table. "Should I take this back?"

"You can leave it," said Louise, "in case Edmund gets hungry later."

Maja nodded and hurried out of the room.

"Where's the hand?" asked Edmund.

Louise gestured to the trolley. "In the bag." As Edmund moved the insulated bag to the dining table next to the place Maja had set for him, Louise crossed the room to where Lucas now stood by Theo's desk.

Lucas pointed to a metal plate attached to the desk. "Viklund put his hand on that to unlock the computer."

Edmund had unzipped the bag and was reaching inside.

"Edmund," Louise said sharply. "Bring it over here."

With a scowl, Edmund brought the bag, hand still undisturbed, to the desk.

Louise didn't intend to cater to Edmund's apparent obsession with Theo's severed hand. She stepped up to the bag, brushing Edmund's arm with hers. As she expected, the intrusion into his personal space caused him to step back.

She lifted the hand out of the bag and removed the plastic wrap. She had handled plenty of dead bodies, first back in medical school and more recently with some of her off-the-books work at Vivantem, but it didn't make the experience any more pleasant. She pressed the hand onto the disc.

The computer screen came to life, and she was about to offer some congratulations to her fellow conspirators, when she noticed the message it displayed:

Biometric signature - Print: Passed
Biometric signature - Temp: Failed
Biometric signature - Heart: Failed

"Shit," muttered Edmund.

Theo's phone buzzed in Louise's pocket. It would be inconvenient for Karl Viklund to pick this exact moment to call. Louise pulled the phone from her pocket and saw that it displayed the same message as the computer screen. She showed the message to Lucas. "An alert for a sign-in attempt."

"As long as it's not alerting anyone else," said Lucas.

"I imagine if it alerted anyone else, it would be you," said Louise.

He pulled out his phone, checked it, and shook his head.

Louise slipped the phone back into her pocket. "I can imagine we can find a way around a temperature check, but what about *heart*?"

"Probably heartbeat," said Edmund.

"Yes, Edmund, I agree," she said with some irritation, "but how do we get around that?"

"Let me give it some thought while we work on the temperature check." He tried to match her tone, but she could tell that having a concrete problem to solve had cheered him up.

They found a thermometer in Theo's bathroom, took the temperature of each of their palms, then brought the hand to the appropriate temperature in a bath of warm water in the sink. They re-tried it on the metal plate.

Biometric signature - Print: Passed
Biometric signature - Temp: Passed
Biometric signature - Heart: Failed

Theo's phone buzzed again. Louise ignored it.

"We might be able to fake it," Edmund said, rubbing his

hands together. "For example, by running a small electrical current that would mimic a pulse through the hand."

Louise glanced at him. "You could do that?"

He looked affronted. "Electrophysiology is my specialty."

"What would you need?"

Edmund began reciting a list of materials, and Lucas pulled his phone from his pocket and thumb-typed notes.

When Edmund had completed the list, Lucas said, "A lot of that should be available in the workshop. If not, Maja or I could go into town to get materials."

Louise supposed she was now in a position to ask Lucas what town that would be. She knew they were in the Catoctin Mountains, near Maryland's border with South Central Pennsylvania. Louise thought back to her earliest visits to the compound, years before. Gerard had accompanied her on her first visit, although he had refused further visits based on Theo's insistence that guests be brought to the compound by his own car and via a circuitous route.

However, she held back her question to Lucas about their location. Considering Edmund's obvious displeasure with the current situation, she didn't want to remind him of the outside world. In any case, until some time in the indeterminate future when she decided it was time to leave the compound, she didn't see that their location made much difference.

Thank you, Lucas," she said. "We should keep the hand cool until Edmund completes his work."

"We can put it in the fridge in the kitchen here," said Edmund, gesturing toward the galley kitchen.

Even though she doubted Edmund could cobble together some kind of re-animation machine with what he could find in the suite, she had no intention of leaving him alone with Theo's computer and the hand. "Keeping the hand cool will certainly extend the time we can use it on the sensor," she said, "but the refrigeration unit in the lab provides finer temperature control. The more closely we can control the environment, the longer we'll be able to use the hand."

Louise didn't actually expect Edmund to believe her reason.

His expression suggested that she was right.

IT WAS late afternoon when Louise accompanied Maja back to the bunker, having received word from Edmund and Lucas that they were ready to test out the electrically re-animated hand on the sensor. Maja had taken advantage of the timing of their visit to load the serving trolley with a tea service and tiered tray of cucumber and watercress sandwiches as well as the hand in its thermal bag.

While Maja lay out tea and Edmund, wielding a small screwdriver, hunched over something at the desk, Louise and Lucas took the hand to the bathroom to re-warm it in the sink. By the time they returned to the main room, Maja was gone. Louise brought the hand to the desk, where Edmund was still fussing with his device: what she guessed was a small generator from which sprouted a tangle of fine wires ending in tiny electrical clips.

"Of course, I haven't been able to test it," said Edmund, "since you had the hand in the lab."

"I don't want to count on having the luxury of iterative testing," Louise said tartly. "We may have a limited number of tries to confirm the last step."

Edmund attached the clips to the hand's exposed muscles and tendons, then turned a knob on the device that looked like it might have been repurposed from a toaster. To the accompaniment of a barely audible electric buzz, a finger twitched.

"Frankenstein," murmured Lucas.

"Frankenstein's *monster*," corrected Edmund.

Lucas rolled his eyes.

Louise lifted the hand, shuddering a bit at the disparity between its lifeless rubberiness and the tiny tremors triggered by the mechanism, and pressed it down onto the disc.

The monitor sprang to life.

Biometric signature - Print: Passed

Biometric signature - Temp: Passed

Biometric signature - Heart: Failed

Theo's phone buzzed in Louise's pocket.

"Turn the current down a bit," said Louise. "Maybe the hand is moving too much."

"Or up," said Lucas. "Maybe it's not enough current to make it seem alive."

"You try holding it," retorted Louise. "It definitely doesn't need to be moving more than it is."

"It might not be the amount of current at all," countered Edmund.

"Try more current," urged Lucas.

Before she could respond, Edmund reached over and turned the knob clockwise. The index finger spasmed.

Biometric signature - Print: Passed

Biometric signature - Temp: Passed

Biometric signature - Heart: Failed

Theo's phone buzzed again.

"*Skit*," groaned Lucas.

"Edmund," spat Louise, "keep your hands off the control until we're agreed on an approach. We don't necessarily have unlimited tries."

Edmund crossed his arms and glowered at her.

"I believe we can agree that the higher current was not the right choice," she said frostily.

Lucas sighed. "Yes."

"And it's not wise to keep trying things willy-nilly, since we don't know how many attempts it will allow us." She arched an eyebrow at Edmund.

"I agree," he said through gritted teeth.

"So I'm going to turn down the current. Are we in agreement?"

Both men nodded.

Louise reached out and tweaked the knob counterclockwise. The spasming finger quieted.

"Maybe we need to take the hand off the sensor first," said Edmund.

"Too late now," she muttered.

She continued turning the knob, millimeter by millimeter, regretting that they hadn't consulted about the need to re-set the sensor between attempts, when she almost gasped as the monitor flashed with a new message.

Biometric signature - Print: Passed
Biometric signature - Temp: Passed
Biometric signature - Heart: Passed

Theo's phone chimed.

Louise smiled. "Well done, Edmund."

Then her smile faded as an empty text box appeared on the screen.

"What?" Edmund bumped her aside to peer at the screen. "A passcode?" He straightened and glared at Lucas. "It needs a passcode, too? You didn't say anything about that."

"I didn't *know* anything about that," Lucas shot back. "I saw him put his hand on the metal plate and then start typing. I had no way of knowing that he was typing a passcode."

Edmund reached for the keyboard. "Should we guess what it is?"

Louise batted his hand away. "Let's not make that mistake a second time. Even if we get three chances at the passcode, we can't just make wild guesses."

Edmund raised his hand to run his fingers through his hair but encountered only the Theo Viklund-style crewcut. He dropped his hand to his side. "And what if there's another authentication behind that? What if there's a retina scan? Think we should be popping ol' Theo's eyeballs out?"

"Don't be hysterical," said Louise. "Lucas said he saw Theo use the handprint sensor and then start typing. There's no reason to think there's more than a password between us and Theo's data." Although, she thought but didn't say, there was also no reason to think that the ever-careful Theo hadn't used multiple passwords. "Let's have Maja come back and remove the hand with the tea service. I'll put it in the lab refrigerator while we decide what to do."

"It's convenient for you that I can't leave this dungeon," Edmund grumbled.

"None of this is convenient for me," Louise snapped.

Lucas glanced between Louise and Edmund. "I'll go get Maja back," he said, and left the suite.

Edmund threw himself into the desk chair.

Louise detached the hand from the device, re-wrapped it in the plastic, and placed it back in the insulated bag. Then she paced the room until Maja arrived a few minutes later to load the tea service and the bag back onto the trolley.

"Thank you, Maja," said Louise. "I'll meet up with you at the lab."

When Maja had gone, Louise turned to Edmund. "Can we at least present a united front to Lucas and Maja? Us bickering isn't helping our cause."

"I'm supposed to be happy about being trapped in here while the rest of you plot out my life? And what's the deal with sending some staff back to Sweden?"

"Edmund," she said, rapidly losing patience, "you know why we're doing that—so that we can eventually replace them with people who don't have a long history with Theo, who are less likely to notice changes to how things are run at the compound."

"So it's all right for people who know every in and out of Theo Viklund's life to go on their merry way, but I have to stay? I hardly saw anything of this place other than the lab and my sumptuous apartment ... at least until you decided to have me masquerade as the master of the house."

She had enough to worry about without Edmund Rinnert's ill-timed whining, but she could hardly afford to alienate one of her three allies at this point. Plus, it seemed clear that she, Lucas, and Maja wouldn't have found a way to pass the biometric check for a heartbeat without Edmund's help.

She drew a deep breath. "Your reappearance in the outside world would raise far too many questions—questions that we can ill afford to be dealing with at the moment."

"Me? I'm just some guy."

Louise restrained herself from pointing out that most of Edmund's complaints had related to his perception that Theo had not treated him with due respect. "You are not 'just some guy.' You are a well-known expert in your field." This was an exaggeration, but perhaps a little flattery would placate Edmund. She gestured toward the device. "How many people could reanimate a severed appendage? Your reappearance after three years would be newsworthy."

He was obviously pleased, but unswayed. "I'd stay under the radar."

"Edmund," she said, trying to keep her tone business-like, "we had an agreement. I agreed to take the blame if our plan went awry—to convince Lucas and Maja that I alone was responsible for Theo's death—and in exchange, you agreed that if things went according to plan, you would stay at the compound to help me manage the situation. The fact that our plan didn't go awry doesn't mean our agreement is void. I expect you to abide by it."

"You want me to help you manage the situation?" he shot back. "Here's a thought: forcing me to stay here might be what makes the situation unmanageable."

Her voice went ice cold. "Edmund. Are you threatening me?"

He crossed his arms. "All I have to do is open that door and tell the guard in the hallway that I'm not Theo and tell him where they can find him." He smirked. "Tell him the *couple* of places they can find him."

She took a step toward him. "You could. Although if the guard in the hallway sees someone other than Theo Viklund —and other than me, Lucas, or Maja—walk out of Theo's suite, I suspect he might shoot first and ask questions later. Furthermore," she took another step toward him, "it's not just me you're threatening. It's Lucas and Maja as well. Do you remember Anders?"

The change of subject caught Edmund by surprise. "No. Who is Anders?"

"He's one of the men who brought me back to the compound when I tried to escape."

Edmund shrugged. "And?"

"Anders isn't at the compound anymore. Well," she amended, "he's still on the property. Or perhaps I should say *under* the property. Six feet under."

Edmund was less skilled at controlling his expression than Lucas was. "He's dead?"

"Yes. Perhaps Anders also wanted to leave the compound." She forced a smile to her lips. "In a way, he got his wish. But unless Lucas and I agree that someone should be released from life at the compound, the only way that will happen is the way it did for Anders."

Edmund stared at her, speechless.

Louise wheeled and strode to the door.

Just as she reached it, he launched one last volley. "You and Lucas are pretty tight, aren't you? Laughing it up in the lab over Theo's dead body. *Literally* over his dead body."

She turned back. "Yes, Edmund, Lucas and I are pretty tight. You'd do well to remember that." She put her hand on the knob. "If you have a clever retort, say it before I open the door. It wouldn't do for the guard to hear a voice that is clearly not Theo's coming from the suite. And all I'd need to do is scream that there's an intruder in here. I wouldn't even need to bother Lucas about it."

She waited a beat, meeting Edmund's wide-eyes stare, then swung the door open, stepped out, and closed the door behind her—perhaps a bit more firmly that she might have had it actually been Theo Viklund in the suite.

QUEEN TAKES PAWN

5

Louise was puttering in the lab after having gotten Theo's hand settled back in the refrigerator when the door opened and Lucas and Maja entered, both a little breathless.

"What is it?" she asked, alarmed. "Has Edmund done something?"

"Not as far as I know," said Lucas. "But the guard at the front gate called. Karl Viklund is there and demanding to be admitted."

Louise's eyebrows rose. "Theo's brother? I assumed he was in Sweden."

"We did as well."

"How does he even know where the compound is? When I visited Theo years ago, I always had to meet a driver miles and miles away, and he took so many turns on the drive here, I couldn't tell where I was."

"Herr Karl was here a long time ago," said Maja, "before Herr Viklund began doing that. He says he'll make trouble if he's not allowed into the compound."

Louise puffed out an exasperated breath. "I wish we didn't

have to deal with an overly concerned brother right now." Although, she had to admit, *overly* concerned wasn't quite right, considering Theo was in the lab freezer. "Should we let him in?"

"I think that's best," said Lucas. "He'll be less trouble for us inside the compound, where at least we can keep an eye on him."

Louise nodded. "That makes sense."

"And he'll want to talk to you as Viklund's second," added Lucas.

She sighed. "Take him to somewhere I can meet with him ..."

"The conservatory," said Maja.

"Yes, that's fine. And I suppose we should have a guest room available for him in case he needs to spend the night." Louise looked at Lucas. "Somewhere we can 'keep an eye on him.'"

"The single room," Lucas said to Maja.

"I'll have it made up," she said.

As Maja slipped out the door, Lucas pulled his phone from his pocket. "I'll drive up to the front gate and pick him up."

"Very good. Please come get me when he's settled in the conservatory." Realizing that that sounded more like an order than a request, she added, "I haven't been to the conservatory. Someone will need to show me the way."

"I'll send Maja back here to get you, and I'll keep an eye on Herr Karl."

He followed Maja out, already talking on his phone.

Maja was back in less than fifteen minutes, and she and Louise returned to the main house. As she followed Maja, she was struck by the fact that "house" seemed hardly an adequate term for Theo Viklund's residence—based on its size, "headquarters" might be more appropriate.

Maja led Louise to a corridor branching off the main hallway, where she saw Lucas standing outside a glass-paned door at its end. As they approached, she caught an earthy aroma and glimpsed greenery through the panes. Maja opened the door and stepped aside to let Louise enter.

The glass ceiling twenty feet above was barely visible through the branches of the carefully pruned trees, and brick walkways wound out of sight through artfully arranged bushes and flower beds. Windowed walls blurred the line between the man-made environment and the natural one. Near the door, the bricks formed a patio area on which stood a cafe table and two metal chairs.

A man was seated on one of the chairs, a jacket draped over its back. At the sounds of the door opening, he stood and turned to face Louise.

Karl Viklund looked like his brother—medium height and slender, with the same iron-gray hair and steel-gray eyes. But his skin was ruddier, and where Theo's hair had been cut with military precision, Karl's was longer, still-thick waves falling over his ears. Rather than Theo's perfectly tailored suits, Karl wore an intricately patterned fisherman's sweater, wool trousers, and sturdy hiking boots. And Karl wore a look of consternation that Louise had never seen on Theo's face.

"Karl," said Louise, extending a hand. "I'm Louise Gerard."

Karl shook her hand. "Pleased to meet you," he said, his tone distracted. His voice, too, was similar to Theo's, but less assured.

Louise waved toward the chairs at the cafe table. "Please have a seat."

Karl remained standing. "I'm here to see Theo."

"As I told you, I'm afraid Theo isn't seeing visitors right now."

"I'm not a visitor—I'm his brother."

"Yes, I realize that. I'm very sorry." After a pause, she asked, "Did you come here all the way from Sweden?"

"No. I flew to the U.S. after Rey's funeral. I wanted to speak with Theo about what he thought had happened to her. I know he has contacts in law enforcement. And after a death, it's only right to be with family." His expression was almost pleading. "Don't you agree?"

"Yes, of course. I completely sympathize with your position, but he's adamant that he's not seeing anyone. He's very distraught."

"*He's* distraught? Rey was *my* daughter!"

Louise raised her hands placatingly. "I know it seems unfair."

"It doesn't seem unfair," said Karl, his voice hoarse. "It seems crazy!"

She was silent.

Karl drew himself up to his full, unimpressive height. "I demand to see my brother."

"I'm sorry. Theo has made it quite clear—"

Karl brushed past her and strode toward the door to the hallway. Just as he reached it, Lucas stepped through into the conservatory.

"*Herr Karl,*" said Lucas, "*jag heter Lukas. Vi träffades för några år sen.*"

"*Theos livvakt,*" said Karl. "*Ja juste, jag kommer ihåg.*" Karl tried to step around Lucas.

Lucas sidestepped to block him. "*Du kunde söka igenom huset och även då inte hitta din brors svit.*" Lucas glanced at Louise and must have noticed her arched eyebrow. He switched to English. "And if you *did* find his suite, there is—at Herr Viklund's express instructions—a guard posted at the door to prevent anyone from entering."

Karl looked between Lucas and Louise, his face a mask of

distress and confusion, and finally settled his gaze on Louise. "I had only two living relatives in the world—my daughter, Rey, and my brother, Theo. Rey has been taken from me—and from what you are saying, she was taking from me in a way that was so upsetting that it drove my brother into seclusion. Now you'd have me understand that Theo is seeing no one except his housekeeper, his bodyguard, and some visitor who happened to be here when Rey died? It's ridiculous!" He looked close to tears.

Maja was hovering in the hallway on the other side of the glass door. Louise gestured her into the conservatory.

"Karl," Louise said in as soothing a tone as she could summon, "can I ask Maja to show you to a guest room while I appeal to Theo to see you? I can't promise anything, but I will ask."

"I can compose my own request," Karl said angrily, "if someone will take a note to Theo for me."

"Of course. Maja can provide some writing materials."

Karl's temper wilted like a punctured balloon. "Unless I'm prepared to battle my way past Theo's security staff, it seems I have little choice."

Louise nodded to Maja.

"Herr Karl," said Maja, lifting his jacket off the chair and draping it over her arm, "if you'll come with me, I'll get you settled in a guest room and provide paper and pen."

Without looking back at Louise, Karl left the conservatory, followed by Maja.

When their steps had receded down the hallway, Lucas said, his tone sardonic, "Perhaps we should have thought up a different story to tell Herr Karl."

"Telling different stories to different people would only lead to complications."

Lucas nodded. After a moment, he said, "If you can get

Herr Karl talking, perhaps you could get some hint about what his brother might have used as a passcode."

She sighed. "Yes. It's worth a try."

"I'll put a man near the guest room—just to make sure Herr Karl doesn't decide to go looking for his brother."

"Good idea."

Lucas started for the door, then turned back. "Herr Karl said Theo and Rey were his only two living relatives."

"Yes."

"He has no family left."

"It sounds that way." Catching Lucas's drift, she added, "Although that doesn't mean he doesn't have friends and colleagues."

"Friends and colleagues in Sweden wouldn't be as likely to investigate a death as family would, especially if it happened on a different continent."

Somewhere in the conservatory, Louise heard the barely audible hiss of a mister turning on, running for a few seconds, and then turning off. "Having two members of a family die unexpectedly within such a short time might also lead to complications."

Lucas shrugged. "I'm merely identifying an option."

After a moment, she nodded curtly. "Yes. We must keep our options open."

WHEN MAJA REPORTED that Karl had finished his dinner, Louise left her suite and made her way to the conservatory. Maja had recalled that Karl and Theo had played chess during Karl's last visit, and a chess board was now set up on the cafe table.

When Louise heard the click of the conservatory door

opening, she turned from her apparent examination of one of the plants. Elsa held the door for Karl, then for Maja, who carried a tray with a bottle in a chiller and two small glasses.

"Good evening, Karl," Louise said. "I trust your room and your dinner were satisfactory?"

"Very nice. Although I'm hoping I won't have to stay there too long before seeing my brother."

"I've spoken with Theo. He's not quite ready to expand his circle of contacts. But," she added hastily, "I'm feeling more optimistic that he might change his mind."

"You gave him my message?"

"Of course. Let's give it another day or two. In the meantime, I hope that we can help you pass the time here enjoyably." She gestured to the chessboard. "I understand from Theo that you enjoy chess. I thought we might play a game."

To Louise's relief, Karl nodded. "Certainly better than spending the evening in my room, comfortable as it is."

"And I see Maja has brought us an after-dinner drink to enjoy with our game."

Maja transferred the bottle and glasses from the tray to the table. "Herr Viklund asked that we serve his brother our finest aquavit."

"Lovely," said Louise. She waved Karl into the chair facing away from the hallway and took the chair opposite.

Maja poured two portions, set them on either side of the chess board, and returned the bottle to the chiller. Elsa held the door as Maja left the conservatory, then followed her out. Elsa disappeared down the hall and Maja took up a position outside the door next to a young man, a member of the security staff.

Louise raised her glass. "Cheers."

Karl raised his glass. "*Skål.*" He tossed back the drink in one swallow.

Louise suppressed a sigh and downed her own drink. Gerard used to tease her about what he framed as their first date, and she framed as a business dinner after her interview to become Vivantem's medical director. According to Gerard, Louise's only signs of intoxication after a cocktail and half a bottle of wine were a slight uptick in enthusiasm when she described her cutting-edge research and a tiny unsteadiness as she made her way to the hotel elevator after wishing him an unequivocal good night. He had been amused that the evening hadn't ended in her bed. That had been many years ago, but she hoped some of her ability to hold her liquor was still in force.

She set her glass aside and gestured to the board, where Karl sat behind the white pieces. "Please begin, Karl."

Karl moved a pawn forward, and Louise did the same.

As play progressed, they discussed Karl's trip from Sweden, previous visits he had made to the U.S. under happier circumstances, and a trip to Uppsala that Louise had made many years ago to give a talk at the university. The news that Louise had visited Sweden prompted Karl to pour another round of drinks. Louise made a mental note to watch out for such moments so that she could be the one to pour— ideally a full glass for Karl and a smaller portion for herself.

Louise had played chess fairly regularly with Gerard, despite the fact that he grew irritable when he lost, so she thought she wouldn't have much trouble dividing her attention between the game and the conversation, but Karl was a skilled player. Fortunately for Louise, he was also a slow player, so she had some time to gather her thoughts on matters related and unrelated to the game while he contemplated his next move.

Moving her rook forward, Louise asked, "What do you do for a living, Karl?"

"Normally I do freelance technical copywriting."

"Normally?"

"Before Rey died, I had decided to take a little sabbatical to focus on birdwatching—it's a bit of a passion for me. I had rented a cottage in the Algarve. That's in southern Portugal."

"Yes, my husband and I took a trip there many years ago."

Concerned that Karl might consider news of another visit by Louise to a European destination worthy of a toast, she poured the aquavit. They raised their glasses and drank.

"So you're married?" asked Karl. "Is your husband also staying with you here?"

Her hand drifted to her wedding ring. "He died recently."

"Oh. I'm so sorry."

He gazed morosely at the board, and Louise took the opportunity to refill his glass. She held the bottle over her glass but didn't pour.

"I had hoped Rey might join me in Portugal," Karl said. "I was never able to interest her in birding, but I think she would have loved the area."

"Do you go birding with a group, or on your own?"

"On my own. I enjoy it as a solitary pastime."

"Does Theo ever accompany you?"

"No. I invited him to go with me once when we were teenagers, but he said he didn't see the point."

Louise nodded toward the board. "How about chess? I suppose you could do that long-distance, each with your own board. Or perhaps on an online forum."

Karl laughed ruefully. "Even when we're together, he only plays when I insist. He's too busy for hobbies."

"Too busy with ..."

"Whatever it he does that enables—" He waved his hand to take in the conservatory, the house, perhaps the grounds as well. "—all this."

"Does he discuss his business with you?"

"No. He's always been quite secretive about it. I understand it has to do with some type of brokerage service."

Brokering power, thought Louise.

"But you said you've been working on a project with Theo," said Karl. "You must know more about his business than I do."

Louise smiled. "Theo is kind enough to fund my research, but I don't believe it has much to do with his business."

"What does your research relate to?"

She moved a piece. "Fitness implications of nonlethal injuries in scorpions. I'm exploring whether tail loss and subsequent constipation decrease the locomotor performance of male and female scorpions."

After a long beat, Karl said, "Scorpion constipation?"

"Yes, it's a fascinating study." She launched into a description of her faux research, gleaned from the website of the Ig Nobel awards, thanks to the phone Lucas had provided. She had chosen the topic on the assumption that it would be boring to Karl—she herself had enjoyed glancing through the referenced papers—but as she regaled him with details memorized and improvised, she realized that suggesting that there were scorpions on the property might provide further incentive for Karl not to go wandering around the house in search of Theo.

When it seemed clear that she had shared enough detail about scorpion anatomy to ensure that Karl would be happy for a change of topic, she steered the conversation to Karl and Theo's childhood in Sweden, then to movies and books Karl had enjoyed and that he thought Theo might enjoy as well. She kept Karl's glass topped up; the level of her own never dropped.

Louise could see that the end of the game was approaching, but she still hadn't heard anything that seemed as if it could provide a hint about what Theo's computer password was.

She wished Gerard was here. He was so much better than she at surreptitiously getting information from people.

She refilled Karl's glass. He was looking blearily at the board, and she didn't even bother pretending to refill her own.

"Rey was so special to Theo," she ventured. "I can't imagine anyone else that Theo might have had a pet name for." She raised her eyebrows encouragingly.

Karl summoned a smile. "He called her *Älskling.*"

"That's lovely. What does it mean?"

"Sort of like *darling.*"

"And how do you spell that?"

Karl spelled it.

Louise cleared her throat, a signal picked up by the bug planted under the table.

After a moment, Theo's phone chimed in her pocket. She pulled it out and glanced at the screen.

Biometric signature - Print: Passed

Biometric signature - Temp: Passed

Biometric signature - Heart: Passed

Theo's severed hand, wielded by Edmund and supervised by Lucas, had passed the biometric authentication.

Enter password.

A moment later, the phone buzzed.

Incorrect password. Two attempts remaining.

Damn. Louise supposed that her hope that they would have unlimited password attempts had been naive. She set the phone next to her empty glass.

"Speaking of pet names," said Louise, "I've known Theo for many years, but I feel I barely know him at all personally. Did he ever have pets?"

"No. Just as he never had any hobbies, he was never interested in pets. I was the animal-lover. Always a dog in tow." Karl waxed nostalgic about his own canine companions, then segued into a description of Rey's love of animals and the long list of the pets his daughter had nurtured over the years. He stopped periodically to dab his eyes with his handkerchief ... and, when Louise poured another serving, to down the aquavit.

Louise concentrated on not accidentally clearing her throat—it was her signal to Edmund and Lucas to try a password, and she didn't want to lose an attempt because of a tickle in her throat. If Theo didn't like animals, he was hardly likely to use the name of one of Karl's or Rey's pets as his password.

When Karl wound down, Louise asked, "And where were you and Theo born?"

"A town near Malmö—Gullvik."

"And how do you spell that?"

Karl spelled it.

Louise cleared her throat, then pretended to consider her next move until Theo's phone buzzed again.

Incorrect password. One attempt remaining.

"Do you need to get that?" asked Karl, gesturing toward the phone.

"No—the calls will stop soon, one way or the other."

"Business?"

"In a manner of speaking."

Karl shook his head. "It's always business with Theo—was even when he was a child." He turned his glass contemplatively on the table. Louise refilled it. "*Tack.*" He downed the drink. "He makes a study of human nature. Always trying to understand what people want."

"That's very generous of him."

Karl laughed sadly. "He doesn't do it to be generous. He does it to gain advantage. He's always been so competitive. Always trying to win. Always trying to best his opponents." His smile faded. "Even people who think they are his friends. Always jousting with them."

Louise's heart skipped a beat. "Jousting?"

Karl roused himself. "Oh, yes. Figuratively, of course. Theo is fascinated by jousting. I sometimes think he would have been happier being born in the Middle Ages. Fancies himself a knight in shining armor, I think." He sighed. "Or perhaps a knight errant."

"A knight trying for the brass ring," said Louise.

Karl raised a finger. "You obviously haven't gotten the lecture from Theo. The brass ring was an invention of carousel-makers. The original rings, the ones used in the medieval jousting fields, were iron."

"An iron ring. Interesting." Her heartbeat accelerated. "And how do you say that in Swedish?"

"*Järnring.*" Anticipating Louise's question, he even spelled it.

Louise cleared her throat.

A quarter of a minute ticked by in silence, then the phone chimed.

Password accepted.

Louise no longer needed to extend the game. She moved her queen past her rook to the last row, where Karl's king stood. "Checkmate."

Karl's eyebrows rose. "Kill box." Karl squeezed the bridge of his nose. "I would have seen that coming if I hadn't had so much to drink."

He knocked his king on its side, leaving a lone white pawn and Louise's black queen and rook on the board.

Louise tucked the phone into her pocket. "Karl, that last

text was from Theo. He wants to speak with me for a moment. I think this is a promising development."

Karl tucked his handkerchief into his pocket. "I'll come, too." He tried to stand but fell back in the chair.

Louise rose. "Please stay here. I sense he's willing to see you, but he's mentioning some logistical considerations he wants to discuss with me first."

Karl passed a hand over his eyes. "Yes, all right."

"Would you like some coffee, Karl?"

He nodded. "Yes, I think that would be a good idea."

Louise raised her hand, and Maja stepped into the conservatory.

"Coffee for Karl, please, Maja."

"Certainly," said Maja.

Louise followed Maja out of the room and approached the guard standing in the hallway. She didn't know his name, or even if he spoke English. "Herr Karl has had a bit too much to drink. If he tries to leave the dining room, please escort him back to his room."

"Yes, Doctor Mortensen," he replied in almost, but not quite, unaccented English.

As Louise hurried down the hallway toward Theo's suite, she thought perhaps the staff who were fluent in English should be the first to be sent away—better not to worry about anyone eavesdropping on her conversations with Lucas, Maja, and Edmund. But it would be easy enough for someone bent on finding out her secrets to pretend not to understand their conversations—just as Anders had when he pretended to be deaf when she climbed into the *AJ's Plumbing* van.

What she really needed, she thought sourly, was a mind reader who could tell her what was really going on behind the bland facades of Theo's staff.

In Theo's suite, Louise found Edmund seated at the dining table and Lucas leaning against the desk, arms crossed.

"What now?" asked Edmund. "Drunk or not, Karl isn't going to leave without seeing Theo." Then he added with a snigger, "And he wouldn't want to see Theo in his current state."

Louise wondered if perhaps *Edmund* had been drinking. She should have had Lucas or Maja check the bunker for alcohol. In any case, if Edmund had found a supply, he was no more obnoxious drunk than sober.

"Lucas will tell Karl that Theo decided he couldn't stay at the compound any longer—the pain of the memory of the times he spent here with Rey, that sort of thing—and that he's gone somewhere else and wants Karl to meet him there."

"What are you going to do when Karl realizes Theo isn't at the other end of the ride?" asked Edmund.

"Lucas will take care of it," said Louise. She turned to Lucas. "Is the car ready?"

"It's at the front entrance."

"And the security camera feed?"

"It's on your phone."

Louise pulled her phone from her pocket. Lucas crossed the room to where she stood, then reached over and tapped a new icon on the Home screen. It showed a grid of four thumbnail-sized videos. He pointed to each of them in turn. "Conservatory. Main hallway. Entrance hall. Front terrace." He straightened his sport coat, nodded to Louise and Edmund, and left the suite.

"You have a phone?" asked Edmund. "That actually works?"

"Yes."

"Why?"

"Scorpion research."

Edmund snorted. "You could have just made that shit up. It's not like Karl is going to know the difference." He stood and peered over Louise's shoulder at the phone. "We're going to watch Karl stumble out?"

"Yes."

She tapped the first thumbnail and the video enlarged to display a view of the conservatory. Maja poured from a silver coffee pot for Karl. She exchanged a few words with him— there was no sound accompanying the video—then stepped offscreen. Karl dropped two sugar cubes into the cup and stirred abstractedly for far longer than it would take to dissolve the cubes.

A minute later, Lucas appeared at the table, a jacket draped over his arm. He spoke to Karl, who brightened. Lucas helped Karl to his feet with a hand on his elbow, then held the jacket for him. It took Karl a few attempts, and some discreet maneuvering by Lucas, to get his arms into the sleeves.

As the two men stepped out of the screen, Louise swiped to the second video feed.

The camera a picked up the pair a few moments later in the main hallway, Karl speaking animatedly, his gesturing arms threatening to upset his balance. Lucas applied a steadying hand to Karl's back.

The third video picked them up as they crossed the entrance hall and stepped outside, where camera 4 showed them crossing the front terrace to a nondescript Toyota SUV. Lucas opened the passenger door for Karl, helped him in, and pressed the door closed before circling to the driver's side and climbing in. There was some movement in the car—Louise guessed that Lucas was helping Karl get his seatbelt fastened —then the car rolled down the drive.

"Wouldn't have wanted to miss that," said Edmund with a yawn. "I understand why we had to get Karl out of the compound, but what *is* Lucas going to do when Karl realizes Theo isn't at the other end of the ride?"

"We obviously can't tell Karl what happened to Theo. We can't keep him here. And we can't send him away to ask questions and raise a fuss."

Edmund looked back down at the phone, where the SUV's taillights were just disappearing into the darkness. "So where is Lucas taking him?"

Louise shrugged. "Anywhere away from here."

Edmund looked up from the phone. "What do you mean?"

"Karl will be the victim of a tragic mugging gone wrong."

Edmund looked from the phone to Louise, the color draining from his face. After a long moment, he asked, his voice unsteady, "Will that work?"

"It will work. It has worked before." Louise thought back to Elizabeth Ballard's father, Patrick, and the faked mugging that her own enforcer, George Millard, had arranged in a filthy alley in Philadelphia.

"But, he's just Viklund's brother. He's just some guy ..."

"It's the ones that are *just some guy* that can pose the greatest threat," said Louise. She dropped the phone into her pocket. "We'll start letting the excess staff go as soon as possible. Once we have a new complement of staff, there'll be no need for you to masquerade as Theo anymore. You can return to your quarters back at the lab."

"I ..."

"Yes?"

Edmund crossed his arms and, although the room was warm, he shivered. "Nothing."

It wasn't only the staff whose minds she would love to be able to read. Her ability to plan her course of action would certainly be improved if she could tell what was going on in Edmund Rinnert's agile but warped mind—or, she thought sourly, if she could just squeeze the life out of him with no fuss and no evidence.

"And when Karl has been taken care of," she continued, "I'll start reviewing Theo's accounts and make sure each of you—Lucas and Maja and you, of course—gets what's coming to you."

THE END

DID you enjoy Kill Box Checkmate? *If you did, I would be so grateful if you would take a moment to leave a rating and review on your favorite online platform. For inspiration, check out what other satisfied readers have said!*

Thank you!

Matty

AUTHOR'S NOTE AND ACKNOWLEDGMENTS

I hope you enjoyed this Louise Mortensen Thriller Novella, which serves as a bridge between Book 3 in the Lizzy Ballard Thriller Series, *The Iron Ring*, and Book 4, *Scare Card*!

Thanks to all those who shared their expertise to bring Louise's story to life:

Robert J. Fischer, (not *that* Bobby Fischer) for sharing his chess expertise.

David Fried, for providing advice on the medical aspects of the story.

Wade Rogers, for providing advice on the scientific aspects of the story.

Daavid Kahn, for providing Swedish translations.

The Ig Nobel Awards, for making available intriguing details of scorpion research.

Jon McGoran, for helping me pull it all together.

Any deviations from strict accuracy—intentional or unintentional—are solely the responsibility of the author.

NEXT IN THE LIZZY BALLARD THRILLER SERIES ...

Lizzy Ballard possesses a dangerous power she struggles to control: the ability to inflict fatal brain injuries using only the power of her mind. Haunted by the memory of her victims, she's on the run from the authorities and from the scientist who created her power, Louise Mortensen.

Lizzy has been hiding out in Arizona with her mentor, ex-con Philip Castillo. She's earning money at the poker tables of Phoenix, thanks to an unexpected ability bestowed by a drug stolen from Mortensen: temporary clairvoyance. When Lizzy and Philip decide to head east to Lizzy's hometown of Philadelphia, she's overjoyed to be reunited with her godfather, Owen McNally, and his brother Andy.

But the East Coast proves to be no refuge when Lizzy is the subject of a brutal attack. Then Mortensen kidnaps Andy and coerces Philip into a lethal game of nerves with her rival, Billy Chapel. Lizzy sees no way out except to comply with the demands of her nemesis.

When Lizzy finds blood stains in Chapel's suite and a dire note from Philip warning her of who the true enemy is, she fears the worse. She demands answers from Chapel, but he's just as baffled as she is. His confusion quickly turns to rage, and he drags her toward Louise's lab—and the final showdown.

Outnumbered but undaunted, Lizzy must rely on her wits and grit to try to outmaneuver Mortensen and Chapel, and to answer the question: can friendship and justice prevail against cruelty and evil?

The only way to win might be to put not just her freedom but her very soul at stake.

Continue Lizzy's adventures in *Scare Card (Book 4)*!

ALSO BY MATTY DALRYMPLE

The Lizzy Ballard Thrillers

Rock Paper Scissors (Book 1)

Snakes and Ladders (Book 2)

The Iron Ring (Book 3)

Kill Box Checkmate (Book 3½)

Scare Card (Book 4)

The Lizzy Ballard Thrillers Ebook Box Set

The Ann Kinnear Suspense Novels

The Sense of Death (Book 1)

The Sense of Reckoning (Book 2)

The Falcon and the Owl (Book 3)

A Furnace for Your Foe (Book 4)

A Serpent's Tooth (Book 5)

Be with the Dead (Book 6)

The Ann Kinnear Suspense Novels Ebook Box Set - Books 1-3

The Ann Kinnear Suspense Shorts

All Deaths Endure

Close These Eyes

May Violets Spring

Ministers of Grace

Our Dancing Days

Sea of Troubles

Stage of Fools

Write in Water

Non-Fiction

Taking the Short Tack: Creating Income and Connecting with Readers Using Short Fiction (with Mark Leslie Lefebvre)

The Indy Author's Guide to Podcasting for Authors: Creating Connections, Community, and Income

ABOUT THE AUTHOR

Matty Dalrymple (DAL-rim-ple) is the author of the Lizzy Ballard Thrillers, beginning with *ROCK PAPER SCISSORS*; the Ann Kinnear Suspense Novels, beginning with *THE SENSE OF DEATH*; and the Ann Kinnear Suspense Shorts, including *CLOSE THESE EYES*. She is a member of International Thriller Writers and Sisters in Crime.

Matty also podcasts, writes, speaks, and consults on the writing craft and the publishing voyage as The Indy Author. She has written books on the business of short fiction and podcasting for authors, and her articles have appeared in *Writer's Digest* magazine. She serves as the Campaigns Manager for the Alliance of Independent Authors.

Matty lives with her husband, Wade Walton, and their dogs in Chester County, Pennsylvania, and enjoys vacationing on Mount Desert Island, Maine, and Sedona, Arizona, and these locations provide the settings for her novels.

Go to www.mattydalrymple.com > About & Contact for more information about Matty's fiction work and to sign up for her occasional email newsletter.

Go to www.theindyauthor.com/ > About & Contact for more information about Matty's non-fiction work and to sign up for her weekly email newsletter.

facebook.com/matty.dalrymple
instagram.com/matty.dalrymple

Cover design: Cristian Cotovan

ISBN-13: 978-1-959882-07-7